STORYTIME COLLECTION

This book belongs to

_____

_____

Autumn
Publishing

Published in 2019
by Autumn Publishing
Cottage Farm
Sywell
NN6 0BJ
www.igloobooks.com

GUA009 0419
2 4 6 8 10 9 7 5 3 1
ISBN 978-1-78905-237-4

Printed and manufactured in China

Disney
Sleeping Beauty

STORYTIME COLLECTION

In a faraway land, long ago, King Stefan and his fair queen longed for a child. Finally, their wish was granted and they had a daughter. They named her Aurora, after the dawn, and she filled their lives with sunshine.

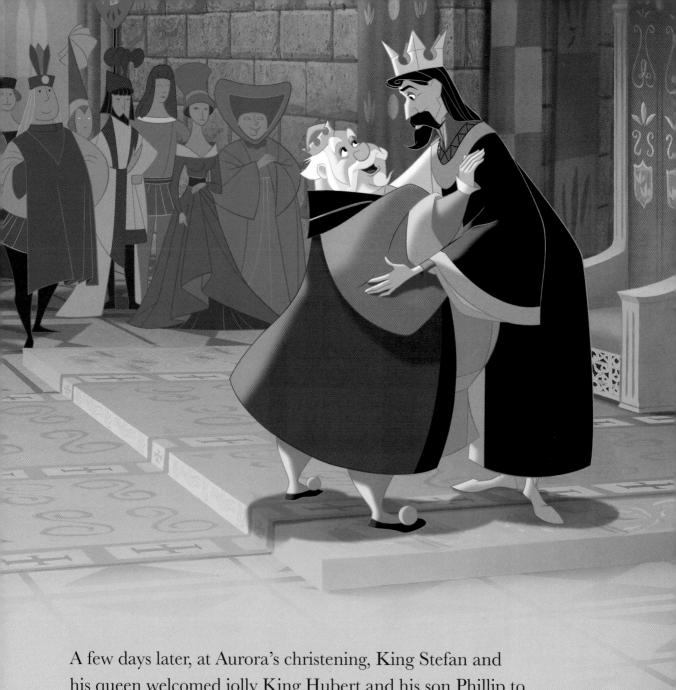

A few days later, at Aurora's christening, King Stefan and
his queen welcomed jolly King Hubert and his son Phillip to
meet the new princess.

The two kings wished to unite their kingdoms and decided
that one day Phillip and Aurora would marry.

Three fairies, Flora, Fauna and Merryweather, arrived at the castle to bestow their gifts upon the baby.

"Little princess," said Flora, waving her wand, "my gift shall be the gift of beauty."

Fauna was next. "Tiny princess, my gift shall be the gift of song," she announced.

Suddenly, just as Merryweather stepped up to the crib, a strong gust of wind swept through the royal hall. There was a flash of lightning and out of a plume of green fire and smoke, the evil Maleficent appeared.

The sorceress was very angry at not being invited to Aurora's christening, so she had a gift of her own for the young princess.

"Listen well, all of you," declared Maleficent. "The princess shall indeed grow in beauty and grace, but before the sun sets on her sixteenth birthday, she shall prick her finger on the spindle of a spinning wheel and die!"

"Seize that creature!" cried King Stefan to the palace guards, but Maleficent laughed and disappeared in another flash of lightning and green flames.

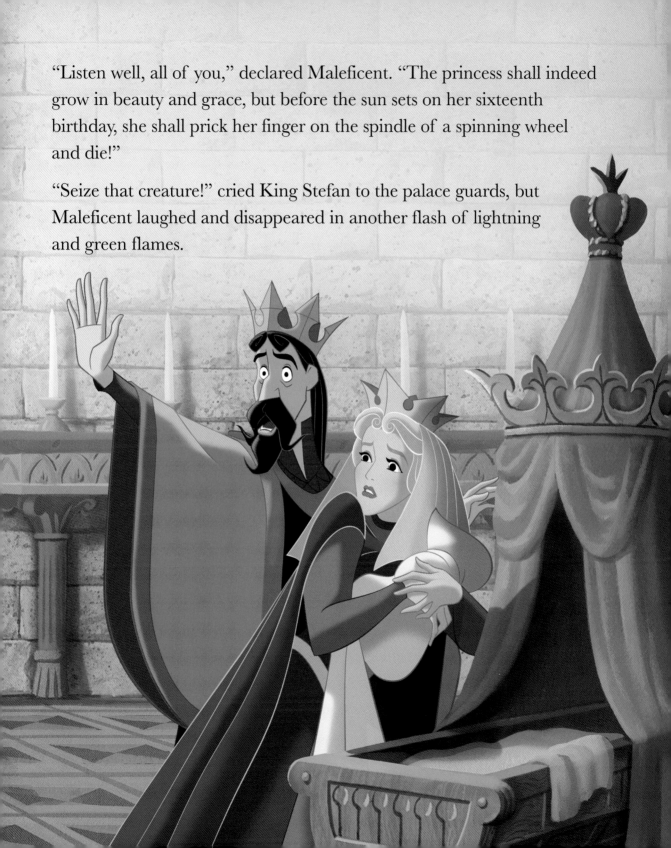

With only Merryweather's magical gift remaining, the curse could only be softened. Merryweather promised that if Aurora pricked her finger, she would not die, but fall into a deep sleep. "You shall wake when true love's kiss the spell shall break," added Merryweather. However, still fearful for his daughter's life, King Stefan had every spinning wheel in the kingdom burned.

The fairies also had a plan to help stop Maleficent from harming Aurora. They would disguise themselves as peasants and raise the princess in an abandoned cottage deep in the forest, with no magic.

The king and queen knew it was for the best, but they watched with heavy hearts as their only child disappeared into the night.

Maleficent and her henchman searched tirelessly for sixteen long years, but never found the princess. If the sorceress didn't find Aurora, the curse might never come true.

So, on the day of Aurora's sixteenth birthday, Maleficent turned to her pet raven. "You are my last hope," she said. "Circle far and wide, search for a maid of sixteen with hair of sunshine gold and lips red as the rose. Go, and do not fail me."

Meanwhile, a beautiful and happy girl named Briar Rose greeted the day
from her cottage window. It was her sixteenth birthday. She did not know
that she was really the Princess Aurora and that her 'aunties' were fairies.

For her birthday, the fairies wanted to surprise Briar Rose with a cake
and a dress – and to tell her the truth about her royal identity.
To get her out of the cottage, they asked her to pick berries in the forest.
"But I picked berries yesterday," said Briar Rose, suspiciously.

"Oh, but we need more, dear,"
said the fairies. "Lots, lots more!"
Briar Rose went on her way, leaving
her 'aunties' to arrange her surprise.

Briar Rose walked through the forest singing a lovely song, and confessed to her animal friends that she had met a handsome prince, but only in her dreams. At that moment, Prince Phillip and his horse, Samson, were riding through the forest when Phillip heard Briar Rose's beautiful singing.

Suddenly, Samson jumped too high and the prince fell in a stream,
becoming soaking wet. He took off his hat, cape and boots so they could
dry, but when Phillip wasn't looking, the animals took them and dressed
up as a make-believe prince. "Your highness," said Briar Rose, laughing
and playing along.

Prince Phillip followed the sound of Briar Rose's beautiful voice and soon found the young woman. Though she was surprised to see the prince at first, Briar Rose then smiled and took his hand. The pair then twirled and danced together just like in one of Briar Rose's dreams.

Phillip and Briar Rose were nestled in each other's arms when, suddenly, Briar Rose realised she needed to get home. "When will I see you again?" asked Phillip.

"Tonight," she replied. "At the cottage in the glen." Neither knew the other's name, only that they had fallen instantly and deeply in love.

Back at the cottage, both the cake and the dress had been disasters.
Merryweather insisted they finally use magic again. "I've had enough of
this nonsense," she said, fetching the wands for the first time in years.

"I think she's right," agreed Fauna, looking at the mess they'd made.

"Here they are, good as new," said Merryweather, waving the wands in the air.

Sure enough, a beautiful dress soon appeared. However, Merryweather and Flora disagreed on its colour and, as the dress kept changing from pink to blue, and back again, the magic struck the cauldron by the fire, sending sparks shooting up the chimney. Just at that moment, Maleficent's raven flew past and saw the sparks. He quickly took off to alert the sorceress.

When Briar Rose returned home, the fairies surprised her with
the dress and cake, but she couldn't wait to tell her 'aunties' about
the wonderful young man she had just met.

"Oh, no," said Fauna. "You are already betrothed to Prince Phillip."

"How could I marry a prince?" asked Briar Rose. "I would have to be a
princess."

"You are dear," replied Flora. "You are Princess Aurora and tonight we
must take you back to your parents."

As the evening approached, Aurora dutifully accompanied
the fairies to the castle, where King Stefan and King Hubert were
already celebrating Aurora's return. However, Aurora's thoughts
were of the young man she had met and fallen in love with that day.

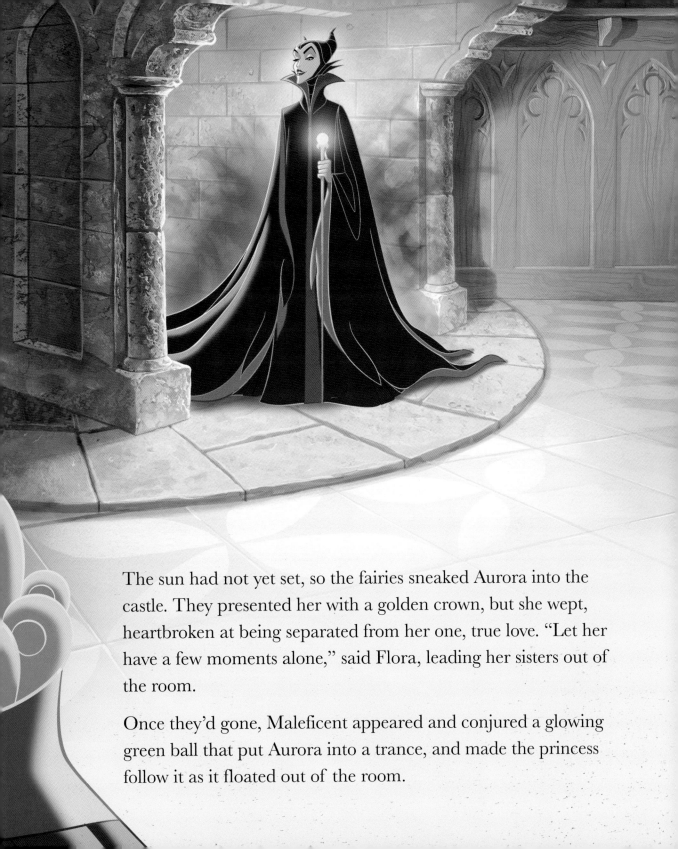

The sun had not yet set, so the fairies sneaked Aurora into the castle. They presented her with a golden crown, but she wept, heartbroken at being separated from her one, true love. "Let her have a few moments alone," said Flora, leading her sisters out of the room.

Once they'd gone, Maleficent appeared and conjured a glowing green ball that put Aurora into a trance, and made the princess follow it as it floated out of the room.

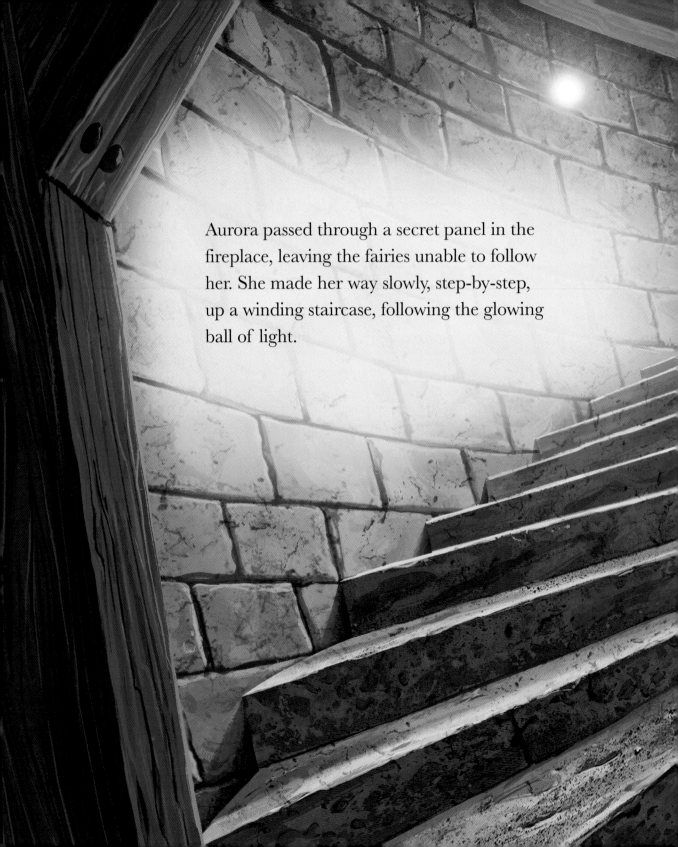

Aurora passed through a secret panel in the fireplace, leaving the fairies unable to follow her. She made her way slowly, step-by-step, up a winding staircase, following the glowing ball of light.

At the top of the staircase, Aurora entered a dark room and came face-to-face with a spinning wheel and a spindle. With her hand held out in front of her, the bewitched Aurora approached the spinning wheel. Maleficent's voice filled the room. "Touch the spindle," she said. "Touch it I say!" Aurora obeyed.

When the fairies finally reached the room, they found Maleficent standing in triumph beside the fallen princess. "You poor simple fools," she said, a cruel smile spreading across her face. "Thinking you could defeat the mistress of evil!" Then, with a wicked laugh, she disappeared.

The three fairies took Aurora to a room in a high tower where they laid her down gently on a bed. Then, they placed a red rose in Aurora's hands as tears ran down their cheeks.

"King Stefan and the Queen will be heartbroken when they find out," sobbed Merryweather.

"They're not going to find out," replied Flora.

Using their magic, the fairies swiftly flew around the castle and placed everyone into a deep sleep until Aurora could wake up again. The fate of everyone in the castle now rested on someone waking the princess.

Back in the forest, as arranged, Phillip and Samson arrived
at the cottage. Inside, Maleficent and her henchmen were waiting.
The evil fairy was not taking any chances that the princess's young man
would save her. The henchmen quickly tied Phillip up. "This is a pleasant
surprise," said Maleficent looking at her prisoner. "I set my trap for a
peasant, and lo' I catch a prince."

Maleficent had Phillip thrown into her dark, cold dungeon
and revealed to him Briar Rose's true identity and her fate.
As soon as Maleficent left, the fairies appeared. They freed
Phillip, then armed him with the Enchanted Shield of
Virtue and the Mighty Sword of Truth. As they rushed up
the dungeon steps, they encountered the raven, who called
out for the henchmen.

With the help of the fairies, Prince Phillip
bravely fought his way out of the castle.
Flora turned boulders into bubbles, and a volley
of sharp arrows into harmless, blue flowers.

Safely away from Maleficent's castle, Samson took
Prince Phillip to find and rescue Aurora.

Determined to keep Phillip from reaching the sleeping princess, Maleficent surrounded King Stefan's castle with a giant wall of thorny bushes. The prince cut through them with the mighty Sword of Truth.

Maleficent was furious. "Now shall you deal with me, my prince," she called, before turning herself into an enormous, fire-breathing dragon. Phillip bravely turned to face the menacing creature. He used the enchanted Shield of Virtue to protect himself and Samson from the heat and force of Maleficent's terrible flames.

The thorny bushes began to burn from Maleficent's fire. With flames rising all around him, Phillip needed to move to higher ground. He climbed up a cliff, as Maleficent charged after him. Raising his sword, Phillip prepared for the battle to continue.

Prince Phillip took aim and valiantly threw his sword, striking Maleficent in the chest. She lunged towards him, but stumbled from her injuries. Phillip scrambled out of the way as the cliff face crumbled and Maleficent fell to her death.

The prince lost no time in getting to Aurora's bedside. He knelt down and gently kissed his true love. Her eyes fluttered open and she smiled at him. The fairies clapped with glee. The spell was broken and the rest of the castle began to wake up, too.

All eyes were on Phillip and Aurora, as they walked down the stairs to the royal hall. They looked so much in love.

"It's Aurora, she's here!" exclaimed King Stefan. The prince and princess bowed before the throne, then Aurora ran to embrace her parents for the first time in sixteen years.

Phillip and Aurora danced, as the kingdom rejoiced.
Together, the prince and princess lived happily ever after.

THE END

COLLECT THEM ALL!

With 12 more exciting titles to choose from, you'll want to complete your Storytime Collection!

Can Aladdin and Jasmine stop the evil Jafar?

Will Bambi learn the value of friendship?

Will Belle be able to break the curse?

Will Dory finally find her parents?

How far will a father go for his son?

Can Anna and Elsa stop an eternal winter?

Will Mowgli defeat Shere Khan?

Will the Incredibles save the day?

Will Simba ever become king?

Will Ariel be able to find her prince in time?

Can Moana restore the heart of Te Fiti?

Will Rapunzel learn who she truly is?